Published by
Robert Frederick Ltd
4 North Parade, Bath, Somerset,
BA1 1LF, United Kingdom

25
BEDTIME
STORIES

Contents

The Wee Island of Loch Noddie

Little Red Mac and his friend Tam O'Tatie walked down by the shores of Loch Noddie.

"I've heard it said," Tam O'Tatie said rather seriously, "that music can bring the Monster out of the Loch!"

So Tam O'Tatie took out his bagpipes and began to play.

While he marched to and fro, playing fit to burst, his friend Little Red Mac kept a sharp look out across the lake, just in case the Monster appeared.

"Piping makes me feel hungry!" said Tam O'Tatie at last, pausing for breath.

"Then let's find a place for a picnic," said Little Red Mac, who always carried a basket full of food wherever he went.

So they waded out to a tiny island which neither of them had ever noticed before.

"This must be a new island," said Little Red Mac as he climbed up the side and got on the top.

"I know a tune called 'The Wee Island Of Loch Noddie,'" said Tam O'Tatie after they had eaten their picnic. "I shall play it for you on the bagpipes."

No sooner had Tam O'Tatie started to play, than the new island slowly sank into the water, and an awful groaning noise came from the loch.

"It must be the Monster!" yelled Little Red Mac as he made for the shore.

"You silly man!" Tam O'Tatie said. "It's my bagpipes!"

. . . now what do you think it was?

Congratulations, Mr Tappit!

"Tomorrow," said Mr Tappit, the toy-maker, "I shall have been making toys for fifty years!" and he locked up his toyshop and went home for tea.

All the toys in the shop overheard what Mr Tappit had said.

"We'll have a party tomorrow," said the baby doll.

"With presents!" said Teddy.

"And fireworks!" cried a shelf full of toys.

"We could have all three!" shouted the wind-up toys. "A party, presents and fireworks!"

"Don't forget a great big cake!" squeaked the tiny clockwork mouse.

"Let's get busy at once," said Teddy, and the toys gathered round.

By next morning, everything was ready.

Mr Tappit unlocked his toyshop as usual and stepped inside . . . and there in the middle of the floor, was the biggest cake he had ever seen.

All of a sudden there was a pop and a loud bang and toys of all shapes and sizes jumped out of the gigantic cake.

Some of them had presents, some of them had cards and one of them was holding a beautiful iced cake.

"Congratulations, Mr Tappit!" all the toys cried as they waved flags and threw streamers.

"What a surprise," laughed Mr Tappit, quite out of breath. "You've made me very happy!"

"We're having fireworks tonight!" squeaked the tiny clockwork mouse as he scampered off to eat his cake.

Silver Lightning

Silver Lightning was the fastest train on the tracks. His engine was shiny silver with blue and red flashes down the side.

On journeys, Silver Lightning sped from city to city so fast that all that people could see when he whizzed past was a blur . . .

"What an amazing train!" the passengers said. "Silver Lightning can drive himself – he doesn't need a driver or a guard!"

"But I do!" cried Silver Lightning, and a big tear rolled down his gleaming paintwork. "I'm so lonely all by myself!"

So the man in charge of the railway found Silver Lightning his own driver and his own guard, who had nothing to do but ride everywhere on the special silver train and keep him happy!

Three Busy Workmen

Three busy workmen were digging a very deep hole in the road, when, quite by accident, their drill hit a water-pipe.

Soon everything was soaking wet and water was spurting in all directions.

"However did that happen?" asked Jim.

"I think it was my fault!" said John.

"Can't be helped," said Joe. "Let's have our lunch!"

So the three busy workmen sat down and opened their lunch-boxes.

"Oh dear!" groaned Jim as he took out rulers and pencils and pens. "I've picked up my little girl's school-case by mistake!"

Then John opened his lunch box and discovered that he'd picked up the wrong case as well – it was packed full of his little boy's school-books.

"I'd better look in mine," laughed Joe, and he began to blush. His wife had handed Joe her make-up case by mistake, with all her lipsticks and hairsprays!

"This means we have no lunch at all!" cried the three busy workmen.

"If you promise to mend the pipe and stop all the water leaking," shouted the man from the sandwich shop nearby, "I'll make lunch for all three of you!" . . . and the three busy workmen did just that!

The Bathroom Battle

Peter's mum was in a hurry one night at bathtime.

She rubbed and scrubbed Peter in double quick time and before he could blink he was washed, dried and tucked up tight in bed . . .

. . . Back in the bathroom, all the toys were left alone on the shelf.

"It's not fair," said the penguin, "no-one has had time to play with us in the bath tonight!"

"Does that mean we shan't get bathed until tomorrow?" quacked the yellow duck.

"I love bath water!" cried the little blue fish. "Especially when it's full of bubbles."

"So do I!" barked the seal. "I hate being dry."

"Then we must do something about it!" the toy sailor said as he stood on the edge of the bath and spoke to them all. "I can turn on the taps, but I need a little help."

"I can use the end of my tail," said the whale. "I'll turn on the hot tap and you can do the cold tap," he told the sailor.

"Plug's in the plug-hole!" said the little blue fish, as he swam quickly out of the way of the hot water.

It wasn't long before the bath was almost full. The seal put his flipper into the water – just to make sure that it wasn't too hot for the toys.

When the penguin gave the signal everyone dived in, and the sailor very

kindly launched the boats and a whole family of ducks into the bath water.

"Let's have bubbles!" sang the whale at the top of his voice.

"Better still," barked the seal as he dived beneath the water, "let's have a bubble battle!"

Pretty soon everywhere was covered in soft white foam. There were big blobs of bubbles on the bathroom walls, and a pool of water all over the floor.

The whale threw a tailful of bubbles at the sailor, and the penguin and the seal filled the sailing boats to the brim.

"Quiet, someone's coming!" yelled the sailor. Quick as a flash, the little blue fish dived down and pulled out the plug.

"This bathroom's been left a mess!" said Peter's dad as he opened the door. "Better get it cleaned up before Mum sees it!"

So he dried all the toys and put them back on the shelf.

The penguin, who was standing next to the seal, gave him a little nudge. "How about another bathroom battle tomorrow night?" he said.

9

Harriet's Wish

"If Harriet wants a playhouse, I shall build her one!" said her dad, quite determined.

So away he hurried to buy lots of wood, and to see if he needed any new tools.

"Are you sure Harriet really wants a playhouse?" mum shouted after him. But dad was already on his way to the timber yard.

It took simply ages to build the playhouse, with dad hammering and banging in nails every time Harriet left the house.

At long last it was finished, and mum and dad called Harriet into the garden to take a look.

Harriet was speechless and held her breath for a very long time, which made her mum look worried.

"I do wish I had a playhouse," said Harriet one day. "Then I could sit inside and just pretend!" and off she went.

"Did you hear that?" whispered her dad.

"I did!" replied Harriet's mum just as quietly.

"Thank you, Daddy, but that's not really what I wanted," said Harriet shaking her head. So she ran indoors and came back with a picture of her playhouse in a book.

"Is that all?" gasped her dad as he fell back into a garden chair.

"I want a playhouse just like that!" said the little girl, and she held up the book . . .

. . . Now Harriet has the playhouse she really wanted - and dad has a brand new tool-shed that he built himself!

The Penguins Join the Party

Chrissy, Sissy and Missy were sisters. They lived with their brother Sidney on an iceberg in the Atlantic Ocean.

One day a ship taking passengers on a cruise stopped right next to the penguin's iceberg.

The people on board the cruise-ship had never seen a penguin before, especially one in a red waistcoat! So they leaned over the side and began to take video films and photographs.

"Do you mind being stared at?" Chrissy, Sissy and Missy asked their brother Sidney.

"Not one bit!" said Sidney as he straightened his bow-tie.

So the four little penguins posed for the cameras until it grew dark.

Late that night, Chrissy, Sissy, Missy and Sidney heard music . . . it came from the brightly lit cruise-ship.

"Come on girls!" said Sidney. "It sounds like a party, so let's join in!"

So Chrissy, Sissy, Missy and Sidney jumped off their iceberg, swam over to the ship and clambered up on deck.

"Welcome aboard!" yelled the captain above the noise. "Today we stared at you, now it's your turn to stare at us. Come and join the party!"

Randolph, the Reindeer

Randolph the Reindeer was extremely shy. While the other reindeer trotted through the trees holding their heads high and tossing their antlers from side to side, Randolph stood quietly nibbling the moss on the ground, with his head down.

"You're too timid, Randolph!" bellowed the other reindeer as they leapt through the woods. "Be a show-off like us!"

But Randolph pretended not to hear – he just went on nibbling the moss on the ground, with his head down.

Then, from beyond the trees came the shouts of children as they tobogganed down the snowy hillside.

"I'd love to join in," sighed Randolph, "But I'm far too shy!"

Then, as Randolph began to nibble the moss on the ground with his head down, he came across a woollen hat. Next he found a mitten, then a long scarf.

All at once, Randolph's nose began to twitch and, without thinking, he held his head high and began to look around . . . there in a clearing on the edge of the trees lay a little boy by the side of his toboggan.

"I've hurt my leg and I can't walk!" the little boy cried.

So Randolph knelt down, and the little boy slipped his arms round the reindeer's neck and climbed on his back.

Very soon he was back home safely, thanks to Randolph.

"You're a hero!" said the little boy.

This made Randolph feel so proud that he lifted up his head and tossed his antlers from side to side just like the other reindeer!

The Baby Birds' Bedtime

It was late afternoon and all the baby birds were practising flying.

"I can fly upside-down!" chirped a young robin.

"Can you dive from the top of the poplar tree, then brake just before you hit the ground?" asked one daring little thrush who had tried it several times.

"Look at us!" cried nine of the tiniest sparrows, as they flew close together overhead.

Just then, a strange little beak and two big eyes appeared from inside the trunk of the poplar tree.

"Hi, everybody!" said a squeaky little voice. "I'm Ollie, can I play with you?"

The baby birds stopped what they were doing at once and gathered around.

"You're new here," chirped the robin.

"Not exactly," Ollie replied. "I live in that hollow tree and I've been here all the time."

"It's getting rather late for you to play," said one of the bluebirds. "Soon it will be dark!"

Poor Ollie looked very disappointed as he had just made so many new friends.

Then, all of a sudden, he thought of a wonderful idea.

"Why not stay over with me tonight?" cried Ollie.

So off flew the little birds and came back wearing pyjamas. (One or two of the really young ones brought their blankets and pillows.)

"It's so exciting," sang the robin. "I've never stayed up all night before!"

At first everything went wonderfully well. The baby birds fluttered in and out of the branches, playing tag in the twilight.

But when darkness fell, they kept
bumping into one another, and the thrush
almost fell off his perch onto the ground
below!

Ollie could see that his new friends were
getting rather tired, so off he flew and came
back with a tray of snacks and nice things
to nibble.

"We're having a midnight feast!"
whispered one of the sparrows,
his head nodding onto his pillow.

Soon all the baby birds were falling
asleep . . . some of them looked really
uncomfortable.

"Why are you still wide awake, Ollie?"
the robin asked drowsily.

"It's because I'm an owl, and we stay up
all night long!" smiled Ollie . . . and he
took all the sleepy little birds back to their
warm nests.

18

Gordon's New House

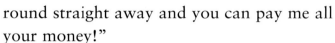

Gordon the Gorilla was looking for a new house. So he rang up the man who sold really nice houses.

"I have the perfect place for you, Mr Gordon," said the man who sold really nice houses. "It has a bright red roof, two tall chimneys and a smart white fence."

"Sounds just the job!" grunted Gordon.

"If you like it, Mr Gordon," said the man who sold really nice houses, "I'll be round straight away and you can pay me all your money!"

As you can see the house turned out to be a bit on the small side for Gordon.

I think that Gordon forgot to tell the man who sold really nice houses that he was a gorilla. Don't you?

Belinda, the Circus Star

"I'm off to join the circus and be a star!" announced Belinda the rag-doll, one morning at breakfast.

"Forever?" gasped the soldier doll.

"No, silly!" Belinda sniffed. "Just for one day."

"One day!" all the toys laughed out loud. "How can you be a circus star in just one day?"

"Easy," said Belinda, "the clowns will teach me, you'll see!" and off she went.

At first the clowns were thrilled to see Belinda, because they thought the rag-doll was charming and very, very pretty, and every single one of the clowns wanted to teach her their tricks.

"But I don't want to do tricks," said Belinda, quite snappy. "I want to walk a tight-rope!"

"A tight-rope?" this surprised all the clowns.

"How about juggling instead?" asked one of them.

"Riding a unicycle is good fun!" suggested another.

Then all the clowns stood in front of Belinda. "We should never allow a beautiful rag-doll like yourself, to swing on a trapeze, or ride bare-back, or walk a tight-rope – it's far too dangerous . . . and that's final!" they shouted.

"Rubbish!" Belinda yelled back as she stamped her feet. "I've already told my friends that I am going to walk a tight-rope and be a star . . . and that's final too!"

Whatever was to be done?

The clowns liked Belinda very much and didn't want to disappoint her, in spite of her bad temper that day.

"There is one way you can learn to walk the tight-rope without being in any danger at all!" said the clown with the big feet.

"Show me! Show me! Do, do, do!" cried Belinda, impatiently . . . and so they did!

Belinda the rag-doll walked up and down the tight-rope all that day. She wore sparkling tights and a silver star on her head . . . and when the toys came to call for her that night, she showed them what she could do. "But Belinda," said the toys, "your tight-rope is only a few inches off the ground!" and they all burst out laughing!

"I agree," and Belinda smiled her prettiest and most charming smile. "But I did learn to walk a tight-rope and I am a circus star!" . . . then she bowed, still wearing her sparkling tights and silver star!

The Bear Who Drove the School Bus

On certain days when the regular driver had a day off, Barnaby would drive the school bus.

Now, on the days when Barnaby drove the bus to school, he picked up his young animal friends at stops all along the forest road.

One day, as his last passenger climbed aboard, Barnaby got back into the driving seat – and the bus would not start.

However hard Barnaby tried, he could not start the engine!

"Hurrah!" yelled one of the raccoon twins. "Let's take the day off!"

So before Barnaby could stop them, all the young animals had jumped off the bus and rushed into the woods to play hide and seek.

"This is very naughty of you all!" shouted Barnaby, trying to sound gruff. "Come back at once!" and his voice echoed through the trees.

All the rest of that morning, poor Barnaby ran round in circles trying to catch the young animals. Every so often he would glimpse a couple of them peeking from behind a tree trunk.

Time passed and Barnaby began to feel hungry. "It must be almost dinner time!" he said out loud.

Then, as if from nowhere, all Barnaby's little animal passengers appeared.

"I'm very hungry!" cried one little fox cub.

"I'm hungry and thirsty too!" said a small squirrel.

"Take us back to school for our dinner!" the animals shouted all at once.

"I might have some food in my bag," said Barnaby, as he led them back to the bus – but all he could find was a packet of cough sweets and some rather old biscuits.

"We want our dinner! We want our dinner!" the hungry animals began to chant, and they banged their feet loudly on the bus floor.

Just at that moment, a big car-transporter drew alongside the school bus.

"Need a lift?" asked the driver.

"I need lots of lifts!" laughed Barnaby.

So Barnaby and the driver put a few of the animals into each car on the transporter.

"First stop school!" shouted the driver.

"Just in time for dinner!" yelled the little animals.

Dottie's in Fashion

Winter was coming and the weather was getting colder, so Dottie the Dormouse went to the store to buy a new coat.

"Choose something sensible that is comfortable and warm," suggested her cousin Dora.

"Not likely!" scoffed Dottie. "My new coat will be the latest fashion!" . . . then Dottie saw it . . . the most fashionable coat in the whole world!

"I'll take it!" Dottie yelled at the top of her voice. "Wrap it up at once!"

"Aren't you going to try it on?" asked her cousin Dora as she gazed open-mouthed at Dottie's new coat. "It looks rather thin!"

But Dottie didn't hear her, she was far too busy trying on a pair of high-heeled boots to match.

"They look very unsuitable for wet,

winter weather!" said Dora under her breath as she followed Dottie out of the store.

During the night it turned very cold. The north wind blew and it started to snow, and it went on snowing and snowing and snowing.

When Dottie and Dora looked out of their window the next morning, the whole world was white.

"Get a move on Dottie!" cried Dora, who was already dressed in her warm jacket and boots.

"I'll need time to button up my coat!" snapped Dottie. "Then it will take me quite a while to lace up my boots!"

So Dora went out to play in the snow with her friends.

At long last Dottie was ready. She stepped outside in her high-heeled fashionable boots and fell flat on her back!

Now Dora and her friends were having a great time throwing snowballs and building a snowman. But the snow was cold and wet, and very soon poor Dottie felt frozen in her fashionable coat.

"It's so c-c-c-cold, and my t-t-t-toes ache!"

"Let's get you inside," said cousin Dora shaking her head. "You need warm clothes on a day like this, not fashionable ones!"

"You're right!" agreed Dottie as she thawed out in front of a warm fire.

"Tomorrow we'll both go shopping and you can choose some sensible clothes for me Dora . . . and I'll pack my fashionable coat and boots away until spring!"

Mat's Morning Coffee

Mat the Bat was feeling lonely. "I need to make new friends," he squeaked as he flitted across the night sky.

"My problem is," he told a passing owl, "each time I introduce myself, everyone screams and runs away!"

"I understand," nodded the owl wisely. "When people see a bat they think of witches and broomsticks and Halloween."

"Got it in one!" piped Mat. "They think of skeletons with rattling bones, and ghosts that jump out at you and shriek and groan!"

"Enough!" hooted the owl. "You're scaring me stiff!"

"Didn't mean too!" said Mat the Bat. "But what can I do?"

"Have a coffee morning!" suggested the owl. "Put a notice on your door inviting anyone passing to come in for coffee and cake. But remember, be sure to have it in the daytime!"

"What a clever old owl you are!" and Mat the Bat smiled as he flitted off home.

. . . Now, when visitors came to Mat's house the next day to join him for coffee and cake – they were in for a surprise.

There was Mat in his neat little house serving coffee and cake in his best frilly apron . . . UPSIDE-DOWN . . . after all, don't forget that Mat's a bat!

Buggy Races

"Would you like to race me down to the beach?" the Hare asked the Tortoise.

"Not really," muttered the Tortoise. "You'll win as usual!"

"That's true," said the Hare in a kind voice. "I'm sorry you always lose, it can't be much fun!"

But one day, the Hare found a way to race the Tortoise that would be fair and lots of fun too.

"Come and look what I have found!" called the Hare to the Tortoise, who was slowly plodding over the sandhill towards the beach.

Now the two friends can race against each other all day . . . and something tells me that the Tortoise might win this time!

The Farmer's Barn

One fine morning in autumn, a farmer and his wife were strolling through the fields looking at their corn crop.

"We've never had such a good harvest, dear!" said the farmer happily. "There'll be plenty of corn for us and all our friends. In fact, there'll be enough left over to feed the birds through the long winter."

"We'll give a party," suggested the farmer's wife. "In fact, my dear, I'll ask my cousins from over the hills and far away."

So the farmer and his wife sent out invitations. Then they got busy in the farmhouse kitchen and made lots of delicious things to eat.

They set the food out in one of their fields under the shade of a tree.

Soon neighbours began to arrive, and last of all came the cousins from over the hills and far away.

It wasn't very long before everyone tucked into the lovely food and seemed to be having a good time.

It was then that the farmer and his wife noticed that the cousins from over the hill and far away looked a bit glum.

"Whatever is the matter?" asked the farmer.

"There must be something wrong with my food!" said the farmer's wife, and she tasted a piece of pie to make sure.

"The food is fine, thank you," the cousins from over the hills and far away replied quietly. "But this year our crops have failed, and we have no corn to eat or save in our barns for winter."

"Don't worry!" cried the farmer. "There's plenty here for all. Take as much as you like home with you, and then come back for more!"

At this, the cousins from over the hills and far away cheered up considerably and began to enjoy the party.

When, at last, the food was finished and all the pots cleared away, the cousins from over the hills and far away took a stroll round the farm . . . and would you believe it, for the second time that day, their faces began to look glum.

"Look at your barns," they said to the farmer and his wife. "They're falling to bits! You'll have nowhere to store your corn this winter!"

Now it was the farmer's turn to look glum.

"Not to worry!" said the cousins from over the hills and far away. "We'll stay a few days and repair your barns for you. It will be our way of saying thank you for giving us the corn!"

The Tired Little Monkey

The smallest monkey at the zoo was very fond of Norah, the zoo-keeper's wife.

"It's because you spoil him so much," the zoo-keeper grinned.

"I can't help it," Norah smiled as she lifted the little monkey up in her arms. "He's so cuddly and sweet, and he's just a baby!"

Now, the little monkey liked nothing better than to follow Norah around all day long as she worked in the zoo.

"Please can you carry me?" the little monkey asked Norah one afternoon. "My legs are tired!"

So for the rest of that afternoon, Norah took the little monkey around the zoo on her back.

"I do like this!" cried the little monkey. "I can see everything from up here, and I'm not a bit tired!"

"But I am!" whispered Norah under her breath – because she didn't want to upset the little monkey.

It took poor Norah twice as long to do all her jobs in the zoo, because the little monkey kept hugging her tightly round the neck and tickling her ears.

"Can we do this every day?" begged the little monkey, and Norah gave a big sigh.

. . . So early next morning the zoo-keeper went into town to buy a pushchair – it was Norah's idea!

So now that little monkey is pushed around the zoo. He never gets tired, and neither does Norah!

Pippin has the Measles

Ma and Pa Bramley were looking rather worried. Pippin, their pet pig, felt poorly.

"Have you been eating green apples from my orchard?" asked Pa.

"Not one!" sniffed poor Pippin.

"Have you been drinking from muddy puddles?" asked Ma, because she had often watched Pippin do this when she thought no one was looking.

"Not this time," moaned Pippin.

"We must send for the doctor," Ma and Pa decided, "he'll be sure to know what's the matter!"

By the time the doctor arrived, Pippin was covered in tiny red spots.

"Measles!" the doctor nodded wisely. "You have a pig with the measles!"

"You must stay in the kitchen with me!" announced Ma Bramley. "Then you will be warm and dry, and I can make sure that you have plenty of warm bread and milk with brown sugar on top!"

Pippin quite liked the sound of this, so she trotted into Ma Bramley's kitchen and settled down in front of the fire.

It wasn't long before Pippin the Pig began to feel a bit better, although she was still covered in bright red sports.

Some of the children in the valley heard about their friend Pippin and came to see how she was feeling.

"It's good to see you all," snuffled Pippin trotting towards the kitchen door.

"STOP RIGHT WHERE YOU ARE!" cried Ma Bramley. "You'll have all these children covered in spots and in no time at all the whole valley will catch the measles!"

"Did the doctor say when I could go out?" asked Pippin.

"Exactly one week from now, and not a moment before!" replied Ma Bramley with a very determined look in her eye.

This news made Pippin look very glum. "Does that mean I can't see my friends for a whole week?" cried the little pig.

"Not at all!" chuckled Pa Bramley as he came in from his orchard.

"I've made you a gate from the branches of an old apple tree. You can stay in the kitchen on one side of the gate, and your friends can stay on the other. That way you'll be happy, and your friends won't catch the measles!"

"We will come and see Pippin every day until her spots have disappeared!" cried the children. "Thanks a lot Pa Bramley!"

Plumber Bear's Good Idea

Nanni Bear was having her breakfast early one morning, when she felt a drop of water fall onto her head, and when she looked up at the ceiling, another one splashed onto her nose.

"There must be a leak in the bathroom!" sighed Nanni as she pushed the teapot into the middle of the table to catch the drips.

"I'll send for Plumber Bear straight away. He'll know what to do!"

When Plumber Bear came at long last, he went straight upstairs. As he walked out of the bathroom he shook his head.

"You need a new bath, a new wash-basin and a new toilet. Your bath is leaking, your wash-basin is cracked and your toilet is very old-fashioned!"

"No wonder," said Nanni Bear, reluctantly, "they must be at least as old as me. I suppose you'd better put in a new bathroom!"

"It will take quite a while," said Plumber Bear. "You never know what I might find!"

So off went Nanni to stay with her sister for a week until the work was done.

When she returned, there was Plumber Bear standing in the garden looking very pleased with himself.

"I know you were fond of your old bathroom so I didn't throw it away," he said, grinning and pointed to a corner of the garden. "Here it is!"

. . . How Nanni Bear laughed when she saw what Plumber Bear had done!

Gussie the Ginger Cat

Gussie the Ginger Cat, made up her mind one day to catch every single mouse in the house.

So she fetched the biggest, tastiest, smelliest piece of cheese she could find and put it inside a bag.

Now, Gussie's bag had a string round the top. "When this bag is full of mice," sniggered Gussie, "I shall pull the string so tightly, that not one of them will escape!"

But what Gussie didn't know was that her bag had a big hole in the bottom.

So one by one, the crafty mice scampered into the bag, picked up the cheese and carried it out through the hole at the other end.

"Better luck next time Gussie!" giggled the mice, their mouths full of tasty cheese.

Huey's Present

Huey the Hairy Caterpillar was looking for a present for his girlfriend.

"Does she like lettuce?" asked a passing ant.

"A lettuce leaf isn't much of a present!" said Huey. "And it's not very romantic!"

"How about a fresh spring onion?" suggested a brightly coloured beetle.

"Now you're just being silly," Huey groaned as he wriggled away.

"Take her one perfect flower!" a butterfly sighed as she fluttered by.

And straight away, Huey knew that was the right idea.

So he picked a beautiful yellow daisy and crawled off to visit his girlfriend.

"How very romantic!" sighed Huey's girlfriend as she gazed at the flower, then they sat together in the warm sun . . . and ate it!

Lolli and Pop's New Car

Lolli and Pop took out all their savings from the bank and bought a new car.

They parked it in front of their garden gate and, for the rest of the day, Lolli and Pop gazed out of the window admiring it.

"Let's go for a ride," said Lolli to Pop next morning. So after breakfast they locked up the house, went down the garden path, Pop got into the driving seat of their shiny new car and turned the key.

"Please start!" said Pop to the little car.

"No!" came the reply.

"Please will you take us for a ride?" Lolli asked.

"Won't!" snapped the car.

Would you believe it . . . every day the same thing happened. However many times Pop tried to start the car, it simply would not budge.

"It's no good," said Lolli to Pop, "we shall just have to stay at home!"

As time went by, Lolli and Pop's shiny new car began to get dirty parked on the dusty road. The tyres were flat and a careless boy on a bike put a dent in the wing. One of the doors was scratched and the bonnet was covered in muddy pawprints made by next door's cat.

"Our little car is only fit for the scrapyard now," said Lolli to Pop as they leaned over the garden gate.

"What's that I hear?" gasped the little car to himself feeling quite shocked. "I've been very stupid parked here sulking all this time. I don't want to be sent to the scrapyard!"

So he tried very hard to start his engine. The little car coughed and spluttered, but try as he might, his engine simply would not start!

Lolli and Pop heard their little car and rushed over to help.

Pop threw open the bonnet and tinkered with the engine. Lolli pumped up the tyres then washed and waxed the paintwork.

"I'm afraid you'll have to go to the garage to have that dent in your wing put right," said Pop.

So the two of them jumped into the little car and Pop turned the key.

"Please start!" said Pop to the little car, and the motor began to tick over at once.

"Please will you take us for a ride?" asked Lolli – and off they raced.